CW00972293

II

DOBBIN AND THE SILVER SHOES

AND OTHER STORIES

This edition published in 2015 by Pikku Publishing
54 Ferry Street
London E14 3DT
www.pikkupublishing.com

ISBN: 978-0-9928050-6-7

First published by the University of London Press Ltd in 1936

Pikku Publishing and Dr Frances Grundy, heir to the estate of
Elizabeth Clark, wish to state that they have used all reasonable
endeavours to establish copyright. If you would like to contact
the Publisher, please write to Pikku Publishing.

1 3 5 7 9 10 8 6 4 2

Printed in China by Toppan Leefung Printing Ltd

"PLEASE TO COME INSIDE, MUM," HE SAID.

(*See page* 13)

[*Frontispiece*

DOBBIN AND THE
SILVER SHOES

AND OTHER STORIES

by

ELIZABETH CLARK

Author of " Twenty Tales for Telling,"
"Tales for Jack and Jane," etc.

Illustrated by

NINA K. BRISLEY

Pikku Publishing ▐◆▬

AUTHOR'S NOTE

The tales in this little book and its companions are reprinted from various collections of stories for storytellers which I have written during the past ten years.

It has been very often suggested to me that children would enjoy reading these stories quite as much as (I am happy to believe) they have hitherto enjoyed hearing them read or told. Accordingly, some of the stories have been chosen.

I hope that these small books may bring pleasure to innumerable small people, at home, at school, or wherever they and the books may be.

ELIZABETH CLARK

CONTENTS

The TALE of DOBBIN and the SILVER SHOES

Chapter One : Poor Dobbin !

IT was a very fine day early in June. The sun was shining, the sky was blue. The hedges were full of dog roses, and the wind blew soft.

But Mistress Mary Jane was walking up and down a field of buttercups and grass and clover, looking at the ground and crying as she walked. Big round tears were running down her cheeks, and she was saying, " I can't see one. Not one. Not even a little one."

She was talking to herself. There was no one else to talk to, except an old white horse standing by the hedge. There was a stout brown rabbit too, but he was hopping up and down the field, taking no notice of Mistress Mary Jane at all.

Mistress Mary Jane lived in the white cottage just across the road. It had a garden full of flowers in front, and a yard full of chickens behind. There was another field with a black and white cow, and a sty with a nice little pig. A tabby cat was washing itself on the cottage doorstep.

Mistress Mary Jane was rosy-cheeked and fat and comfortable. You would have thought she had everything in the world to make her happy that fine sunshiny day. Yet here she was crying, and the old white horse looked as unhappy as she did.

The trouble was that the old white horse had gone lame. He had been all right only the evening before, but when Mistress Mary Jane came into his field in the morning he could hardly move. His mane and his tail were full of tangles, and he looked as if some-one had galloped him far and fast.

To-morrow Mistress Mary Jane was to go to a village ten miles away for her brother John's wedding. She had a new bonnet with cherry ribbons, and a new sprigged muslin gown. There were a pot of honey, three pounds of fresh butter, and some new-laid eggs, all ready to be packed in a basket. At eight o'clock Mistress Mary Jane had meant to climb on to Dobbin's broad back and go jogging away with her basket on her arm, down the green lanes to the wedding.

Now Dobbin was lame.

Mistress Mary Jane was quite sure it was the Fairies who had been galloping him round the field all night. There was a great fairy ring in the middle of the field, so she knew the Good Folk came there.

She was hunting up and down the field for a four-leaf clover, for she knew that if you can find a four-leaf clover, the Fairies cannot play tricks with you. If only she could find one she meant to go to the fairy ring that night.

She was going to give the Fairies a good talking to, and tell them that they must cure Dobbin of his lameness before the next morning.

But she could not find a four-leaf clover. It seemed there was not one in the whole green field. Mistress Mary Jane's back ached. Her temper ached. She was hot, and tired, and cross, and disappointed. That was why she was crying.

Just then a very big tear rolled down her cheek and fell splash in the middle of a clover leaf.

Mistress Mary Jane looked down.

" I do believe that is a four-leaf one," she said.

But when she stooped and picked it, it was not a four-leaf. It was a five-leaf clover; and as she stood looking at it, a very odd thing happened.

Chapter Two : Mr. Rabbit Talks

THE stout brown rabbit stopped hopping up and down the field and nibbling at the grass and clover. Suddenly he turned round and came hopping across the field to Mistress Mary Jane. When he reached her, he sat and looked at her. There was a four-leaf clover hanging out of his mouth. Then a still odder thing happened. The stout brown rabbit began to talk.

" At your service, Mum," he said. " Please to take the clover."

Mistress Mary Jane stooped down and took it.

" Where ever did you find it ? " she said. " I couldn't see one."

That was the only thing she could find to say. She was so very surprised.

" I have been eat-ing them all the morning," said the stout brown rabbit. " I am caretaker of this field, Mum. I had my orders to eat every four-leaf clover before you could find it.

But the Good Folk forgot that it is Leap Year. If you find a five-leaf clover in Leap Year you can come and go as you like for twenty-four hours, by day *or* by night. Elves, Pixies, Fairies, Good Folk—none of them can stop you. So if I were you, Mum, I should come here after sunset this evening and talk to the Little Folk. Bring both the clovers with you, and you will get what you want."

"Thank you. So I will," said Mistress Mary Jane.

She had stopped being surprised. It seemed quite natural to be talking to a rabbit. Perhaps it was because of the five-leaf clover.

She went over to the old white horse and patted him. Then she went back to her cottage, and put the clover leaves in water, and had her dinner. Afterwards she finished trimming her bonnet with cherry ribbons, and packed the butter and honey and eggs. She was quite sure everything was going to be all right now that she had her clover leaves.

The sun does not set till past nine in June. So about half-past nine Mistress Mary Jane went across the road to the field with both her clovers safe in her hand. It was still quite light. She could see old Dobbin standing with his ears pricked up, watching the fairy ring.

Mistress Mary Jane could see nobody, but the stout brown rabbit was waiting for her.

" Please to come inside, Mum," he said, and hopped inside the ring.

Mistress Mary Jane stepped after him. She could still see nobody, but the grass blades all round the ring were shaking and quivering, though there was not a breath of wind. The stout brown rabbit seemed to be listening to something she could not hear. She could see his ears twitching. Presently he said :

" They want to know, Mum, if you will have the old horse nimble and quick or steady and strong ? "

" Steady and strong," said Mistress Mary Jane in a great hurry. She was thinking of the butter and eggs, and her own fat comfortable self.

As she spoke, it was like throwing a stone

into a still pool. You know how the ripples spread and spread. The grass blades quivered and shook, and all round the ring she could hear clear little voices.

" Steady and strong," they said. " Steady and strong, steady and strong, steady and strong."

The tiny voices grew fainter and fainter and fainter. Farther and farther away they went, till all was quiet again.

" That's all right, Mum," said the stout brown rabbit. " Now, if I were you, I should just go home to bed."

So she did. She slept soundly till the birds woke up and began to talk to each other at daybreak.

" Bless me," said Mistress Mary Jane as she woke, " it is brother John's wedding day."

Then she remembered about Dobbin and the Fairies, and she jumped out of bed and looked out.

The sun was not up, but the sky was golden in the east, and pale clear blue overhead. She could see Dobbin in his field. He seemed to be standing in the fairy ring. Mistress Mary Jane bustled about and put on her lilac print dress. It was too early to dress for the wedding, of course. She put on a pair of clogs.

" The meadow will be sopped with dew," she said.

Last of all she picked up her clover leaves, and hurried down the garden path and across the road. As she reached the gate of the field, the stout brown rabbit popped out of the hedge to meet her.

" Please to come this way, Mum," he said.

Then he hopped across the field in front of her to the fairy ring. There stood Dobbin.

" Oh ! " said Mistress Mary Jane. " Oh, Dobbin ! "

Chapter Three : Off to the Wedding

DOBBIN was a sight to see. His mane and his tail were like white silk, so glossy and bright. His coat was like the finest white satin, and he was shod with four new beautiful silver shoes.

" There he is, mum," said the stout brown rabbit proudly. " Steady and strong he is, and just fit for a wedding."

" Yes, indeed," said Mistress Mary Jane.

Then she went and stood by Dobbin in the fairy ring, and picked up her lilac print skirts, and dropped a very deep curtsey.

" Thank you kindly, all Good Folk," she said. " Thank you, with all my heart."

" You are very welcome, mum," said the stout brown rabbit. The grass blades round the ring quivered and shook, and Mistress Mary Jane could hear clear little voices. " Welcome, welcome, welcome, welcome," they said.

From farther and farther away they came, just like spreading ripples on a pond. Then a little wind came rustling across the meadow, and a long ray of sunlight came with it. The sun was up, and all the dewdrops sparkled and shone and danced. Mistress Mary Jane could see her shadow lying long and dark on the bright green grass, and Dobbin's too.

The stout brown rabbit was nibbling grass and clover, with his little shadow beside him. He did not seem to have any more to say, so Mistress Mary Jane went back to the gate with Dobbin following her. His lameness had quite gone. He seemed as steady and strong as anyone could wish. She patted his shining coat and went back to her kitchen.

When she had milked the cow, and fed the chickens and the little black pig, and given the cat a saucer of milk and eaten her own breakfast, Mistress Mary Jane dressed herself in the sprigged muslin and the bonnet with cherry ribbons. Then she climbed on to Dobbin's back with her basket of eggs and honey and butter.

Away they went through the green lanes to the wedding. When she got there, everyone said that Dobbin was the handsomest horse that ever they had seen, with his silver-shining shoes.

Nobody knows what the shoes were made of, but they never wore out. For many and many a day Mistress Mary Jane and Dobbin jogged along together, steady and strong.

As for the rabbit, Mistress Mary Jane often saw him hopping about the field, but he never spoke to her again. The clover-leaf magic lasted only for twenty-four hours, you see. She pressed the leaves in a fat book, and sometimes when her neighbours came in for a cup of tea she let them have a peep at it. Then she told them the story of the four-leaf clover and the five-leaf clover, and Dobbin's silver-shining shoes.

THE LITTLE SILVER BELL

Chapter One : The Lonely Island

ALL up and down the coast of Norway there are scores and scores of islands. They are little and lonely, and not much will grow on them except grass and heath and furze.

Because they are so little and lonely the fairies stayed there a very long time after they left all other places. Fairies like to give presents to anyone who pleases and helps them, and that is what happens in this tale.

There was once a boy named John who fed his sheep on a green heath on one of these little islands. There were some great mounds near by, which folks called the Giants' Graves. It was said that the fairies lived there and that they danced by moonlight on the green grass.

But nobody knew for certain, for no one but John cared to go there, for fear of vexing the fairies. John had no fear of them. Besides, he had nowhere else to go.

John lived with his sister Elsa in a tumbledown cottage near the Giants' Graves. They had no father and mother. All they had in the world was the cottage, a stony little field of rye, and a tiny flock of sheep. John dug and sowed and reaped the field, and took care of the sheep. Elsa spun and wove the wool from the flock, and looked after the home. Sometimes they sold a sheep, and so they made enough to live on.

But it was a dull life. John wanted to go to school to learn, as other boys did. He wanted to be good to Elsa and to keep her from working so hard. He wanted a great many things, but it seemed as if he would have to stay on the island and take care of the sheep all his life.

So the time went by till the day came on which this story happened.

It was Midsummer Day, very early in the morning; the sun had scarcely risen, and the grass was still wet with dew. As John wandered after his flock among the Giants' Graves, he saw something bright and shining lying on a very smooth green little patch of grass. He ran to see what it could be.

Chapter Two : The Blue Bird

THERE on the grass lay a little silver bell. It was no bigger than a thimble, and

it had marks like queer writing round the edge. John picked it up and rang it softly. It gave the sweetest sound he had ever heard. It was like sunlight, and shining water, and the song of birds, all in one clear note.

As the sheep heard the little bell they stopped nibbling and lifted up their heads and came trotting nearer to listen.

" This must be a fairy bell," said John, and he rang it again and again. Then he sat down by a furze bush and hung the little bell on a long green thorn, and listened while it tinkled softly in the wind.

All day long he sat listening as he watched his sheep, and it seemed to him the loveliest and the shortest day he had ever known. Everything seemed friendly : the gulls, the rabbits, the little brown birds that pop in and out among the furze bushes, the plovers and the field mice. None of them seemed afraid. They came and went, and listened fearlessly to the chiming of the little silver bell.

" It must surely be a fairy bell," he said again.

John was quite right. It was a fairy bell. If a fairy loses his little red cap or his tiny red shoes as he dances, he must work very hard till he gets another pair. But to lose his little silver bell is far worse ; for then he must seek and search and never go back to fairyland until he finds it.

Now the fairy who had lost this bell had danced fast and far the night before. Over land and sea he danced, over clouds and mountains and tree-tops.

He was very worried when he found that the bell was gone, and he changed himself to a shining blue bird and flew about looking for it.

All day he looked with his bright eyes, but  he never could find the little silver bell. The day was long, for it was Midsummer-tide, when the sun hardly goes to sleep at all in Norway. The fairy bird's wings were weary, and he was feeling very frightened and lonely as sunset drew near.

"DOWN FROM THE SKY DROPPED THE SHINING BLUE BIRD."

24]

Just as he was giving up hope he saw a little green island in the blue sea. There sat a shepherd lad by the side of a furze bush. Round him the white sheep were feeding, and the sheep bells tinkled softly as they moved.

But clear above the sheep bells the fairy bird could hear another bell ringing. As he flew he answered it and sang :

" Sweet ring the sheep bells ;
  No bell have I.
Till the lost is found again,
  Far must I fly.
Sweet ring the sheep bells,
  But none is so dear
As my lost silver bell
  That rings so clear."

John looked up.
" What a strange sweet bird ! " he said. " Will it come to me as the sheep did if I ring ? I will try."

Chapter Three : The Little Fairy Man

JOHN rang the silver bell softly, and down from the sky dropped the shining blue bird. It flew into a dark green furze bush, all golden in the sunset-light.

John ran to the bush. He thought, " Perhaps its nest is there."

But the low sun dazzled his eyes, and before he reached the bush he was surprised to see an old woman coming towards him.

" My son," she said, " that is a very sweet bell of yours. Will you sell it to me for my little grandson ? I will give you three silver dollars for it."

" Nay, mother," said John, " three dollars will not buy it. Listen how sweet it is. When I ring it, my sheep follow me as I will."

" I will give you five dollars," said the old

woman eagerly. " I will give you a handful. I will give you gold. I must have the bell."

" Nay, nay, mother," said John. " Gold does not ring like my silver bell."

Then he rubbed his eyes, for suddenly the old woman was gone. In her place stood a tiny man in a red cap, a green coat, and little pointed shoes. He hopped nimbly to the top of a big rock and tugged at John's coat.

" John," said the fairy man. " Oh, John, be a good lad and give me back my silver bell. I have searched for it all day long. The sun is nearly set, and I cannot go back to fairyland without it."

" So that is it, little neighbour," said John. " Well, it is a merry bell, and I shall miss it sadly; but I would not keep it from you. So take the bell, and good luck go with you."

As he spoke the sun dipped behind a low

cloud, and the light went out like a candle. The fairy was gone, and the silver bell with him. But on the ground at John's feet lay a shepherd's crook. It was made of white wood, carved with wonderful little pictures of woolly sheep and lambs skipping and dancing, and flowers and little peeping fairy faces.

John took up the fairy crook and went home with all his sheep trotting willingly behind him. He had a wonderful tale to tell Elsa that evening.

From that day the fairy folk brought him good fortune. His sheep grew fine and fat, their wool was thick and soft and white. There were no such sheep to be found in all the countryside.

John grew rich, but he was always kind. In time he had a large farm and built himself a great house, where he and Elsa stayed till they both married. They and their families lived happily ever after, and for many a day men showed strangers the house, and told the story of the fairy crook.

Chapter One : Mrs. Wren's Find

ONCE upon a time there was a little house that stood by the seashore. It was so small that all it held was a heap of dry branches and fern for a bed, and a log for a seat. It was built of grey stone piled together without mortar. The roof was of boughs thatched with golden-brown reeds from the marshes near, and it had neither a chimney nor a door.

But outside the little grey house there was a gay little garden, and at the time the story happened it was very gay indeed. There were yellow and brown wallflowers, smelling sweet in the sunshine. There were big yellow double daffodils and little blue hyacinths, and other flowers too many to tell.

The little honey-bees hummed and the big bumble-bees buzzed in and out, and the man who lived in the little grey house sang to himself as he worked in the garden.

His name was St. Malo, and this story happened so long ago that nobody knows very much about him. But we do know that he came from Britain to teach the poor people of Brittany. It was in Brittany, just where the town of St. Malo stands now, that he built his tiny house and made his gay little garden.

St. Malo was very busy in his garden that spring morning. There was so much to be done. A little rose bush had nearly been blown away by the winds from the sea. That must be tied up. The weeds were coming up thick among the flowers, and the grass was trying to choke them. All that must be cleared away. Then there were the vines in his little vineyard to be tied up to strong sticks driven deep into the earth.

St. Malo worked hard, and the spring sun was hot. Presently he took off his long brown robe, with its pointed hood that he pulled over his head in cold wet weather, and hung it up on the bough of a tree. Then he went on with his work.

A little while after, two small brown wrens came flying into the garden. Wrens are tiny birds, but they have quite big voices, and these wrens were talking very loud indeed.

" My dear," said Father Wren, " I cannot think why you won't settle this year. The blackbirds and the thrushes and the starlings are all building, and the swallows will be here soon, yet we have not even chosen a place. You know it is quite time we began to build."

" Well," said Mrs. Wren, in a high, shrill chirp, " you must remember, Father Wren, that I am the one who has to sit on the nest. It is all very well for you. You can fly about, but I must find a really snug place to sit. I have not seen anything that pleases me yet."

Mrs. Wren suddenly chirped. " What is that over there ? " she said.

Then with a quick little flit and flutter she flew off. Where do you think she went ?

She flew straight into the pointed brown hood of St. Malo's robe as it hung on the bough of the tree. She dived right down to the very bottom, and Father Wren heard her giving little surprised chirps of delight.

"So soft," said Mrs. Wren, "so warm, so sheltered, so well hidden! I shall certainly stay here in this beautiful nest I have found."

Father Wren began to say, "You can't stay there, my dear," but Mrs. Wren stopped him.

"It is not the least use your talking like that, Father Wren. Go and find me something to eat. All this has made me quite hungry."

Father Wren knew it was no use to talk. Mrs. Wren was a sweet little brown bird, but when she made up her mind she would not budge. So he flew away, talking to himself.

"It won't do to build in those brown feathers hanging on that tree." He meant

St. Malo's robe. Of course he thought all clothes were feathers. "They belong to that two-legged person who is scratching and pecking about this place. Mother Wren will be very much surprised and upset when he comes to take them away. But it is no use my talking. I will go and find something for her to eat. She will need it."

So Father Wren flew away, and came back and busily fed Mother Wren. The wall-flowers and the daffodils nodded in the wind, the bees buzzed among the flowers, and St. Malo worked away in his garden.

All the time Mother Wren sat quiet, tucked away deep down in the bottom of St. Malo's hood. The sun sank lower and lower in the blue sky, and presently the bees went home to bed. St. Malo stood up and stretched himself.

"That is enough for to-day," he said. "The wind grows cold. Night comes, and soon it will be time to rest."

He went over to where his brown robe hung on the branch of the tree. He stretched out his hand to take it, but he had scarcely touched it when there was a little chirp. Out of the hood fluttered a tiny bundle of brown feathers. It was poor little Mrs. Wren.

Chapter Two : Happy Mrs. Wren

" Oh dear ! Oh dear, Father Wren ! " Mrs. Wren twittered, " you were quite right. Those beautiful brown feather things belong to that two-legged person after all, and it has come to take them away. Oh ! I never was so upset in all my life. What will become of my beautiful egg ? "

Father Wren was as worried as Mother Wren. But he need not have been, for what do you think St. Malo did ? He stood still for a minute, holding the brown robe very carefully, just a little surprised. Then he smiled, and put his hand into the hood and felt about into its farthest corner. Presently he found a tiny egg.

It was so tiny that most people would have been afraid to touch it. But St. Malo loved

flowers, and so he knew how to be gentle with all tiny things. He took the tiny egg out and looked at it. Mother Wren was quite right. It was a beautiful egg, about the size of the tip of his little finger. It was pinky white, all powdered with tiny red spots.

Father and Mother Wren were terribly worried, poor dears, but still they need not have been. St. Malo looked very kindly at the egg for a moment. Then he put it back into the hood, and hung the robe again on the bough of the tree.

" Little Mother Wren has more need of it than I," said St. Malo.

He went into his little house, and had his supper of dry bread and water, and said his prayers, and went to sleep.

Outside in the garden little Mother Wren

settled down gladly on her beautiful egg, and
Father Wren sang a loud thank-you song.
Then he too went to sleep with his head under
his little brown wing.

So there the hood hung, all through the
weeks that followed. Sometimes there was
rain, and sometimes the wind blew stormy
and cold. St. Malo must have missed his
warm woollen robe, but he left it hanging on
the bough, and never thought of taking it
away. He knew about the little family that
lived there, and he watched Father and
Mother Wren fly in and out feeding them.

There were a great many baby wrens, quite
ten or twelve. At last they peeped out and
learned to flutter about the garden. After
that they all flew away. Not till then did
kind St. Malo take down his robe from the
bough where it had hung so long to make a
home for Father Wren and Mother Wren and
all their fluffy family.

Nowadays there is a busy town on the place
where St. Malo's little house stood and his
garden and vineyard grew. Tne vineyard

is gone long, long ago, and there are families of boys and girls in the town instead of families of wrens. But St. Malo is not forgotten, for the town is called by his name; and in the country round you will find plenty of people who can tell you the story of the saint who was so kind to little Father and Mother Wren.

Chapter One : The Beggar Man

HAVE you ever heard someone say, " I met with Good Luck to-day "?   It all sounds rather as if " Good Luck " were a kind of person, and something like that is what people used to believe, as this story tells.

Once upon a time, many years ago, old Mrs. Featherfuss was standing at her garden gate. She was a large stout person with white hair and a very clean white apron.

The house was very clean and white too. The stones of her garden path were as white as stones could possibly be, and so were the palings of her garden. It was a very tidy garden. There were no flowers in it, but there was a row of parsley down each side of the path, and there were neat rows of vegetables : carrots with feathery tops turning red and golden-yellow, dark crimson beetroot, stout green cabbages, and shining celery.

Old Mrs. Featherfuss looked as if she liked good things to eat, and so she did. As she stood there she was thinking of the little black pig in the sty at the back of her house, and how fat he was growing, and how good he would taste with sage and onions and apple sauce.

" But I must not stand here wasting time," she said to herself. " I must go and make up the fire and see about my tea."

Just as she was turning from the gate an old beggar man came hobbling down the road. He seemed very lame and very tired. Old Mrs. Featherfuss hurried up the path for fear he should ask for something.

" I have got enough to do to look after myself," said she.

The beggar stopped a moment and leaned against the palings as if he would like a rest, but Mrs. Featherfuss bustled round the corner of her house and into the kitchen by the back door. She shut the door with a very loud slam, and began to poke up her fire to boil the kettle to make a cup of tea. The beggar man shook his head, and sighed, and went on down the road.

There was another house a little farther on, a very tiny one. It had a thatched roof that came low down, just like a comfortable old hat pulled over somebody's head. A rose bush grew on one side of the door and a red fuchsia on the other. They almost hid the front of the tiny house, and its little windows peeped out like two bright eyes. There was a cabbage patch on one side of the garden path, and on the other side there were flowers : Michaelmas daisies, buttony brown chrysanthemums, and pink and blue asters.

"COULD YOU SPARE A POOR OLD MAN A BIT OF BREAD
AND CHEESE?"

Chapter Two : From Sunset to Moon-time

As the beggar came down the road an old woman in a blue-checked apron came out of the little house. Her name was Betsy Pink-pottle and she lived there all alone with her big tabby cat for company. Her face was all brown and rosy and wrinkled like a little old apple, and her brown eyes twinkled very kindly.

The beggar man looked at her and nodded his head as if he saw something pleasant.

" Good evening, missus," he said. " Could you spare a poor old man a bit of bread and cheese ? "

Betsy's eyes twinkled more than ever.

" I can give you something better than that," she said. " I have got no cheese, but what would you say to a fine large rosy apple ? I had three beautiful ones given to me to-day. I was just going to have one for my tea, and you are welcome to one too. Indeed you are."

She trotted into the kitchen, and came out again with a large red apple and a big slice of bread on a blue and white plate. The beggar man thanked her, and settled down on an old tree trunk by the side of the road to eat.

Presently he came to the door. It was standing wide open, and Betsy was sitting at the table finishing her tea.

" Here is the plate, missus," said he. " My thanks to you ; and may what you begin at sunset go on till moon-time, without stop or stay."

Then he went hobbling down the road. Betsy came to the door and stood watching him and wondering what he meant.

" The sun is setting, sure enough," she said to herself, " but there is nought to be done but tidy the kitchen. What should I be doing till moon-time ? "

She stepped back into the house, and picked up the apple that was left, and put it on the shelf. Then she turned again to clear away the tea things. But there was still an apple on the table.

" Bless me ! " said Betsy. " Where did that come from ? "

It was large and round and red and shining. Betsy touched it. It was certainly a real apple; and as it was on her kitchen table it must certainly belong to her, so she put it on the shelf beside the other. They looked very nice sitting there,

and Betsy admired them with her head on one side. When she turned round there was another apple on the table in the very same place, a beautiful streaky red and yellow one.

" Well, I never did ! " said Betsy, and she picked it up and put it by the side of the other two.

" Three lovely apples ! " she said, and so they were ; when she looked at the table again, there was a fourth all ready for her, just as round and as rosy as the other three.

43

After that there was another and another. Betsy went on for a whole hour taking apples off the table and putting them on her kitchen shelves. There were rows and rows of them. Her arm was really beginning to ache, when at last she turned round and found no apple on the table.

"Well," said Betsy, "that is the last. Where they came from I don't understand, but a beautiful lot of apples they are."

Then she thought of the beggar man's saying : "May what you begin at sunset go on till moon-time." She opened the door and looked out ; and there, low down in the sky, was the tiniest newest new moon that was ever seen. Betsy dropped three curtseys to it, as her grandmother had taught her.

"From sunset to moon-time," she said. "Those apples came from the beggar man. Good Luck has surely come my way to-day ! "

The next morning Betsy Pinkpottle was busy trotting round to all her neighbours, giving a red apple here and another one there, and telling the tale of the wonderful beggar.

Everyone said, " Well, you did have Good Luck yesterday, I'm sure ! " and everyone was pleased—except old Mrs. Featherfuss. She was very angry.

" To think," she said, " that I saw him coming down the road and never asked him in ! If he comes this way again, he shall come to me—and I shall get something better than a lot of apples, I'll be bound."

So every afternoon she stood at her garden gate, with her clean white apron on, waiting for the lame beggar to come down the road. One day, about two weeks later, he came.

Chapter Three :
The Plan that
Went Wrong

MRS. FEATHERFUSS bustled out to meet the beggar man. She invited him to come in and take something to eat. She hurried

him up the path and in at the front door. She sat him down in the best armchair in the parlour.

Then she gave him plum cake, and bread and cheese, and bread and butter, and bread and jam, and a mug of cider to drink. She sat by him and thought what a large meal he was eating, and counted up in her mind all she hoped to get in return. Presently he got up to go. Mrs. Featherfuss showed him politely to the door, and there he said, " Thank you, mistress. Good evening to you, and may what you begin at sunset go on till moon-time, with never a stop nor stay."

Then he hobbled down the path and away.

Old Mrs. Featherfuss turned back into the house. It was just sunset.

" I must be quick," she said. " There is not much time before moon-rise. It is a good thing I put the money ready." And she looked at the fat bag of shillings and sixpences, half-crowns and florins, standing on the table.

" All I need to do is just to open it and pour out the silver. It will go on pouring out till

46

moon-rise, and I shall be a rich woman by that time."

It was a beautiful plan, and perhaps it would have succeeded quite well if she had not upset the jug of cider in her hurry to seize the bag.

" Dear, dear ! " said Mrs. Featherfuss. " What a terrible mess ! "

She snatched up a cloth and began to mop up the cider. There seemed to be a great deal of it.

" I never thought that jug held so much," she said.

She wiped and mopped, and still the cider dripped and poured on to the parlour floor. She ran and fetched another cloth and a pail from the kitchen. The parlour floor seemed to be swimming in cider by the time she got back. The carpet was soaked, and there was a stream running down the passage into the kitchen.

" Dear, dear, *dear* ! What a terrible mess ! " said old Mrs. Featherfuss.

She put the pail by the table to catch the cider, and ran back to the kitchen to fetch her

long-handled mop. Just as she got there the cider stopped running, and old Mrs. Featherfuss, with the mop in her hand and a very red face, stood staring through the kitchen window at a large round full moon that was just rising out of a bank of grey mist beyond the fields and hedges.

" From sunset to moon-time ! " she said. " And all I have got is a spoiled parlour carpet and a pailful of cider ! "

That was all she ever did get. It took her most of the night to clean up the house, and the parlour carpet was never quite the same again.

A LEGEND OF CHRISTMAS EVE

Chapter One : The Crib in the Forest

HERE is an old tale which they tell in Brittany. It is a story of Christmas Eve, of two little children who fed their father's sheep on the edge of a great dark forest.

Their names were Jean and Marie, and they lived with their father and mother on a farm. It was a very little farm. There was a low grey house of rough stones, with some tiny fields of oats and rye, and some cabbages and turnips. There were chickens and pigs and a few sheep. The father worked in the fields, the mother helped him and looked after the

49

home and chickens and pigs, and Jean and Marie took care of the little flock of sheep.

Every morning their mother would give them some bread and cheese and pat them on the shoulder.

" Be good, my little ones," she said, and Jean and Marie nodded their heads and smiled. Then they and the sheep went happily off to the wide open space of heath and grass and bracken on the edge of the forest. There they stayed all day. Marie would spin, and Jean carved rough wooden spoons and bowls and plates for the house, while the sheep fed round them on the moorland.

On sunny days in the spring and summer and early autumn that was a pleasant way to spend the time. When it rained and the wind blew stormily from the sea, there was always shelter in the forest, with its great old oaks and beeches and its thickets of thorn and holly. Even in winter it was not too bad. They could make a fire then, and warm their hands when the frost pinched and the wind blew cold.

But the days that Jean and Marie feared were those when the grey fog came rolling in from the sea. One could hardly see from tree to tree, and everything was so still, except for the calling of the sheep and the drip drip drip from the boughs.

On those days they watched and listened, and were afraid at every rustle in the forest. Their mother was glad to see them safely home, and their father said anxiously, " The Grey Ones have not troubled you, my children ? "

The Grey Ones were the great grey wolves that lived deep in the forest and only dared come near to houses and homes when the thick fog hid them. Then, sometimes, they would come creeping and snatch a sheep from the flock and be gone again ; and what could a little boy or girl do to stop them ? But there was no one else to take care of the sheep, so day by day Jean and Marie went out with them and brought them back each night.

There came a day in December. It was

Christmas Eve. The morning was still and clear and cold, but the mother felt worried as she looked towards the west.

" There will be fog before evening, I fear," she said. " See that you are warm, my children."

So Jean took his great knitted scarf, and Marie was warmly wrapped in a big shawl. Just as they were starting their mother called them back.

" These are because it is Christmas Eve," she said, and she filled their hands with chestnuts and apples to roast at their little fire.

That was pleasant to think about ; but it was not of apples and nuts that Jean and Marie talked as they went along with their sheep. There was something else that they meant to do first. They had been planning it for a long while.

" This night," said Marie, " Jesus was born in the stable at Bethlehem in a nest among the warm hay. To-day we will make a crib in the great hollow oak on the edge of the forest. We will make a soft nest there such as the Baby Jesus had, and make it beautiful."

So when the flock was feeding quietly, Jean and Marie gathered dry grass and soft green moss and red-brown bracken, and they filled the hollow in the old oak tree till it was like a deep soft bed. Then they laid green sprays of ivy round it, and bright red rose-berries and golden-brown oak-apples and crimson haws. It was a beautiful crib, and when it was finished they called the sheep together that they might see it too. " Because, you know, Marie," said Jean, " the sheep heard the angel as well as the shepherds on Christmas Eve, and so they also knew of the stable at Bethlehem."

So they all looked together, and then the sheep went back to nibble the green grass, and

Jean and Marie lit their fire. When it was warm and glowing they put flat stones round it and laid the chestnuts and apples to roast. Presently they would be warm to hold and very good to eat.

Then the fog came.

Chapter Two : The Fog Comes

MARIE and Jean had been so busy that they hardly noticed that the sunlight was growing pale and dim. Suddenly there was a wet cold breath in the air, and the fog came rolling in from the sea, hiding the sun and sky and covering everything in folds of thick

 grey mist. Soon they could see nothing but the great oak tree and the bushes near, and the blaze of their little fire. The flock moved closer in, and Jean and Marie watched

them and talked to each other. They were very glad of the hot chestnuts.

The time went by, and still the fog hung close about them. It was very still.

" Never have I seen such a fog," said Jean, shivering a little in the cold air. " It is on such a day that the Grey Ones come. Listen, Marie ! What is that ? "

As he spoke there was a frightened bleating from the sheep and a quick pattering rush. Then three grey beasts, larger than the largest sheep-dog, sprang from the thick bushes. Each seized a sheep and tossed it over its shoulder. Then, as quickly as they came, they were gone into the forest again.

The frightened sheep came crowding round. Marie began to cry, and Jean could hardly keep from crying too.

" The poor little sheep ! " sobbed Marie. " The Grey Ones have taken them, and we cannot help them. How sorry Father will be." The two poor children held each other tight and crouched down by the fire, shivering with fear and cold.

Presently Marie lifted her head.

"Jean!" she whispered. "Listen! Some-one is coming."

There was a little rustling sound among the dry dead leaves of the forest.

"I am frightened," said Marie. "Is it the wolves again?"

But it was not the wolves. It was a child who came out of the dark forest—quite a tiny child, all in white, with golden hair that seemed to shine in the grey fog. He shivered in the cold air. His hair was rough with silvery drops of mist, and his little hands and feet were bare.

"Oh, you poor little one!" said Marie. "Have you lost your way? How cold you are! Come and be warm."

She took the little child and cuddled him in her arms, and held his hands and feet to the fire. By and by he was warmer, and she wrapped him in her shawl, just as her mother had wrapped her that morning, and laid him in the crib in the hollow oak.

"Here is a soft nest for you," said Marie,

" OH, YOU POOR LITTLE ONE," SAID MARIE, "HAVE YOU
LOST YOUR WAY ? "

and Jean covered him warmly with his big woollen scarf.

The little one snuggled down and seemed to sleep, and Jean and Marie piled more wood on the fire and sat close to it. The fog was like a cold grey wall round them. They were shivering and miserable, and they could not keep from crying as they thought of the three lost sheep.

Suddenly Jean looked up.

" Is it the sun ? " he said.

But it was not the sun. It was a light like sunshine, but it came from the hollow oak. It seemed to shine round the little child they had tucked up safe and warm in the bed of moss and bracken.

He was sitting up and smiling, and he was no longer pinched and cold, but rosy and warm. As Marie lifted him out of the hollow, the child

57

held out his little hands to her and to Jean, and turned towards the forest by the way he came.

They went with him, away from the warm fire into the dark forest. They were not at all afraid to go. They were not afraid to leave the sheep. They each held fast to a hand of the little child, and went where he led them.

It seemed as if the way was plain, even in the thick mist. The thorn bushes and the long trails of brambles seemed to draw aside to let them pass, and soon they came to a stable.

Chapter Three : The Lonely Stable

IT was a very old stable, built of rough logs all covered with grey moss. Jean and Marie knew the forest well, but they could not remember seeing it before.

The door stood open wide and they passed in. There was a manger there, and in the manger there was a bed. It was just such a bed as they had made in the hollow oak, all warm and soft with moss and dried grass and bracken. Kneeling round the manger there were shepherds and many little shepherd boys and girls. Jean and Marie could never say how many there were, for as they looked the stable seemed as large as the world and as high as the sky.

By the light that shone round the little child they saw three sheep that rubbed softly against them with their warm woolly coats.

" Oh, see, Jean," cried Marie. " See our little sheep ! "

The child smiled at them, and the light was

so bright that they were dazzled and closed their eyes.

When they opened them again they were alone. There was no stable, only the forest with the big grey oak trees and dark thorn bushes and shining green hollies. But close to them stood their three little sheep, all warm and soft and well.

Jean and Marie took them back to the flock. When they reached the edge of the forest, they could see the low red sun shining through the mist, and by its light they gathered the sheep and went home.

There they told the wonderful tale of the lost sheep and the little child.

" Surely it was the Christ-child Himself,"

said the mother. " Is He not the Shepherd of the sheep, and does He not love and remember all faithful shepherds like those who came to the stable ? "

Jean and Marie nodded.

" He loves the sheep too," they said.

" Yes," their mother answered. " He is the Good Shepherd. He cares for all the world."

QUESTIONS

The Tale of Dobbin and the Silver Shoes (page 7)

1. Who was to be married, and where did he live ?
2. What was Mistress Mary taking to him ?
3. Why was she more pleased with a five-leaf clover than a four-leaf ?
4. Draw a picture map of Mistress Mary's house and fields.
5. How was she dressed first thing in the morning, and later on ? Look at the pictures, and be as exact as possible ?

The Little Silver Bell (page 20)

1. Where did John live ? See if you can find the country on the map.
2. What is the colour of furze bloom ?
3. What did John want to do that you do ?
4. Draw the fairy bell.
5. What is the use of a shepherd's crook ? Draw one.
6. How was the Old Woman dressed, and the Fairy Man ? Draw him and fill in colours as you think.

The Home in the Hood (page 29)

1. From what country did St. Malo come ? To what country did he go ? What for ?
2. What was his hobby ? What is yours ?
3. Draw a wren sitting on a match-box.
4. About how many eggs does a wren lay, and what are they like ? Paint a picture of one.
5. Pretend that you are St. Malo looking out of your door on a warm April morning. Say what you see. (The picture on page 29 will help you.)

Good Luck and Mrs. Featherfuss (page 38)

1. What was the difference between the two gardens ?

2. The two old women would not have changed gardens. Why not ?

3. Draw what Mrs. Pinkpottle had for company.

4. Mrs. Featherfuss gave the beggar man the better meal of the two. Why did she not get the better reward ?

5. If someone said to you what the beggar man said to Mrs. Pinkpottle, what would you choose to do ?

6. Look at the pictures, and think over these :

Is the story supposed to happen a very very long time ago, or not so very long ? How do you know ?

In the picture on page 45, have they got into the garden yet, or not ? How can you tell ?

A Legend of Christmas Eve (page 49)

1. What did the mother and father do for a living ?

2. Draw a Grey One and write its proper name underneath.

3. What were the children's Christmas Eve presents ?

4. What did the children find in the forest, and what did they do with it ?

5. Look at the pictures. How did Breton boys and girls dress ? Are there any parts of their dress that you like better than yours ? Which—and why ? Are there any things about it that you would like to borrow ? Which—and why ?

6. Even if you did not know that Jean and Marie were not very rich, there is a little thing in the picture on page 52 would tell you. What is it ?